Worlds Apart
by
Francis E Evans

ISBN: 978-0-9926563-0-0

Worlds Apart
by
Francis E Evans

ISBN: 978-0-9926563-0-

Published by

i2i Publishing. Manchester.
www.i2ipublishing.co.uk

Dedication:

To my wonderful family

Francis

"There is always one moment in childhood when the door opens and lets the future in."
Graham Greene

Chapter 1

'Gordon…Gordon... Can you hear?... Do you think?.. Gordon. Oh please. Sue...Do you? What time was it? Peter...it's three hours since. Sue...no thank you. Do you? Don't... darling. Oh please God... Sshh Sue... be OK.'

Words and more words! Hollow flat monotones that, at first seemed no more than far off whispers rising and falling like waves out on a distant ocean, they then came crashing over me like jetsam brought in on some mountainous tsunami. Time and again I found myself floundering in them. Sometimes it was the same word repeated over and over and at other times I could make out half-meaningful phrases. Although there was something vaguely familiar about the voices, their familiarity brought no comfort. On the contrary I found the quiet urgency and the fearful tone that drifted in with them deeply disturbing.

Intermingled with all of this, and somehow integral to it, like some weird modernist symphony, there were other sounds – whirring, clicking and rhythmic tinny sounds. And there were lights too – pinpoint flashing lights, dim pulsating lights, sometimes in synchrony with the sounds, other times not.

It's not that I was thinking as such, nothing as purposeful as that. It would be more accurate perhaps to say that I was simply the passive receptor of it all with neither the understanding nor any motivation to question the events.

Then out of this confusing mélange, there began to emerge some semblance of order. It was rather like the way in which a picture would appear in the very early days of television as you carefully tuned it in. On to the screen, which is at first covered with dancing points of light there would slowly develop a grainy image and eventually a picture.

I saw two boys. They were playing, laughing and running around in the country by a river. And then it changed. There were still two boys but they were much older and they were just standing under an enormous tree talking quietly. Then one of them slowly and very casually leaned back against the trunk of the tree. His face was set like stone and his gaze fixed way into the distance. The other boy began to gesticulate wildly as he spoke, apparently pleading with the gazer who showed not the slightest concern.

Perhaps the most recurrent image though, was that of the face of a young woman. She just stared at me with unblinking inscrutable eyes. I was sure that I knew her and that she was in some way special to me, but the connection eluded me. The final image that I can recall was of the same young woman but now looking directly at me with warmth in her eyes and on her lips the promise of a smile. But then her features changed; her eyes narrowed and her lips curled, baring her teeth, almost snarling. She looked barely human any more. Her mouth opened and such an outburst of anger and loathing spewed from it that I must have jumped with the shock of it.

I opened my eyes suddenly and gasped for air. My body lurched and I felt a stab of excruciating pain in my stomach. I collapsed and lay back breathing hard, willing the pain to go away and still reeling from the effect of that image which had barely faded. Gradually the pain subsided and as it did so I opened my eyes once more and, turning my head nervously from side to side, surveyed my surroundings.

I was faced with a rather drab and dimly lit room. Was it early morning or early evening light that drifted in through the single window to my right? Whichever it was it must have been an uninspiring day outside of these walls. A long fluorescent light tube hung from the ceiling above me on dusty chains. On the wall directly facing me there was a sink and to the left of that a door. I was in some kind of large cot with side rails between which ran a number of tubes and wires linking me to a battery of machines which were just visible if I craned my neck a little further. And it was these, I now realized, that were the source of the sounds and flashing lights that had been woven into those images of my half conscious state.

So there I was, I concluded, lying in a hospital bed and judging by the pain that I had just experienced, quite seriously injured. Despite that painful episode, with a little careful shifting of my body, I was soon able to regain a modicum of comfort. I looked at the clock on the wall - three twenty. It could have been a summer morning or an autumn afternoon. Not that it mattered that much, but there is something slightly reassuring in knowing what time of day it is. Do I have a day ahead in which all will be revealed as to why I am here, or several more sleeplessness hours of uncertainty? Strange to think now considering the circumstances in which I found myself, but I didn't feel any fear or panic as I deliberated over these things.

Then I began to think about what I'd experienced whilst I was coming round; the scenes of the boys playing and especially the young woman. As I did so, more and more became clear to me and although there was somewhere deep within me a quiet but insistent voice telling me not to pursue it, I felt compelled to go with it.

Chapter 2

My memory takes me back to when I was about five or six years of age and to one night in particular. Going to bed was for me, as for all children of that age I would bet, rather a waste of precious play time. But it was part of a routine that my parents had in their wisdom initiated from day one, for my own good I'm sure but equally for the sake of their own sanity. Anyway as I lay there in my bed and drifted into that in-between stage where anything seems possible I felt my body become weightless and I started to rise from the mattress. I floated effortlessly through the ceiling of my bedroom and the roof of the house. I can remember even now the wonderful feeling as I slowly glided up towards the clouds. At one point, when I was perhaps fifteen, twenty houses high I rolled over onto my front and looked down. I saw the river that, from this height, looked like a silver ribbon meandering among the factories and mills with their smoke belching chimneys; and row upon row of back to back terraced houses lining a spider's web network of narrow streets and backstreets. And there were larger shop-lined roads with buses and cars moving noiselessly along like in some old silent film. I could just make out the street where I lived and see my friends playing ant-like below; it was amazing. Higher and higher I went until I was actually among the clouds, big fluffy white ones – the kind that prompt the imagination of children into seeing all manner of wonderful and bizarre creatures. And there I stopped and hovered. I could turn this way and that just by thinking about it. The air was absolutely still and the sun was warm on my skin. It was so quiet - quite magical in fact.

Then I saw something out of the corner of my eye; it was on the same level as me but it was a long way off. It soon became apparent however that it was heading towards me and at some speed, and in the blinking of an eye it was no more than a few feet away. At first I was too shocked to do anything other than flinch at the prospect of being hit by the thing but then I looked closely at it and to my great surprise I saw that it was a child but curled up like a new born baby. Slowly it began to uncurl and as it lifted its head I could see that it was a little boy. But his features were unlike any I'd ever seen before except perhaps on a doll. His hair shimmered in the clear light like finely spun platinum and his skin had the quality of porcelain; as for his eyes, they were huge and steely blue. I could barely stand to look at them, they were so piercing. If he hadn't moved I would have taken him to be a doll – he just looked too perfect. The whole thing lasted no more than a minute and before I knew it the child began to curl up once more and then sped off as fast as he had approached. As far as I can recall I got up next morning and gave no further thought to it. However the same thing happened again about a week later and again a few days later still. In fact, and it suddenly becomes clear to me now, it happened many times over the next few years, sometimes being interwoven with other dreams, other times not.

Then the encounters with the child changed quite dramatically. Up until this point the experience always began in the same way - in that timeless, drifting, not awake yet not quite asleep period. This stopped abruptly and I thought that it was the end of the whole thing after several weeks went by with no contact whatsoever. It seemed strange going to sleep and having normal dreams; and to be honest a part of me was sad to have lost this now so familiar and strangely comforting friendship. I say friendship because even though nothing fresh ever happened, a kind of understanding seemed to have developed between us in spite of the total lack of interaction.

Then one memorable night in June of the year I turned eight I went to bed and went to sleep as soon as my head touched the pillow. This in itself was unusual because I always seemed to spend some time going over the events of the day at school. Anyway it was a deep sleep and I had just the one dream.

In the dream I was standing by a stream sur-rounded by green fields and gently undulating hills – the epitome of the classic English land-scape. But, as in all dreams, there was something not quite right about it. It wasn't a ridiculous or nightmarish thing as is so often the case; it was simply the scale of everything. The colours were of such intensity and brilliance that they almost hurt my eyes, and as for the landscape, it seemed that I could see beyond the horizon, that in fact there was no horizon, the land just went on and on and I was looking into the infinite. Yet here and there, scattered across this vista and belying the surreal nature of what lay before me, I could see perfectly normal, believable features - a hedgerow, typical of any rural scene; a rustic wooden fence and five bar gate; a copse of beech or hazel and the odd mature sycamore and oak tree. The sun was high in an almost cloudless sky and the only sounds that broke the silence were the bell-like tinkling of a nearby stream and the unmistakable song of a skylark. .

There was something very special about that place, the unutterable beauty, the stillness and peace, things that could not be put into words, all contributed to my state of breathless wonder and for some moments I could not move a muscle. The word that comes to mind now that best de-scribed what I felt then is anointing, I had re-ceived an anointing of...of...I still can't say exactly, perhaps the glory that is creation, if that doesn't sound too fanciful.

Then suddenly I felt as though the anointing was withdrawn and I was released from the paralysis that had gripped me, as if I had been prepared for and was now strong enough to withstand whatever was to come. I looked down at where I was standing, now not more than a foot away from the edge of the stream. Kneeling down I slid my fingers into the fast flowing water. It was icy cold and felt more like a torrent of tiny crystals sending sharp, almost painful sensations through my wrist and up into my arm. At the same time warm, earthy aromas mixed with the fragrance of the flowers filled my nostrils and I felt again, only to a lesser degree, something of the awesome force of that place.

I rose to my feet on rather shaky legs, turned and looked around me. That first impression of being able to see for ever had gone and the scene assumed a more normal perspective. The ground rose to an embankment on top of, and running the full length of which was a dense thicket of gorse, heavy with cadmium yellow blossom. I walked steadily up towards the hedge and carefully picked my way between the thorn covered limbs. Once clear of the bushes and with only minor scratches I emerged onto a wide rocky plateau which bore hardly any vegetation save for one enormous oak tree. I could see beyond the tree that the ground fell away forming one side of a massive shallow valley that must have been a mile or so across. My inclination in the real world would probably have been to explore further into the valley but I felt strangely drawn to the tree. It may have had something to do with the fact that, from that rugged dead looking patch of rock emerged this giant - this great, monstrous tree with its huge limbs outstretched high and wide, commanding, aloof, a thing set apart.

As I walked towards it a cool, still darkness enfolded me and once beneath the great cathedral-like canopy of its branches I was in total silence. There was something about that place that yet again touched me deeply; another magical place in a world where magic is almost common place. I decided to retrace my steps and explore further afield but as I turned towards the perimeter of the canopy I noticed what appeared to be the figure of a person – a boy to be more precise. He was so close to the tree that at first glance, in the low light he appeared to be part of the gnarled trunk. I could make out that he had his back to me and seemed to be just staring out across the valley. Part of me wanted to creep away unseen but another part was intrigued. Somewhere deep inside me there was a distant echo. My curiosity won and I began making my way slowly towards the tree. In spite of my best efforts to make as quiet an approach as possible, I stood on a twig which snapped with a loud crack. I froze, my heart thudding so hard I felt sure he would hear that too. He began to peel himself away from the tree like a great chunk of bark. He turned and looked straight at me. For what seemed like ages we both stood there staring, neither of us it seemed, willing or able to move. As the seconds ticked away the echo that had hatched in my mind just moments ago grew louder and louder; that hair, those features, especially those eyes. There was now no shadow of doubt; it, or rather he was that baby but now so much more grown up. And what's more, at that very same moment I somehow knew that he too recognized me. Our eyes were locked and like two statues we faced one another for what seemed like an eternity. To this day I can't recall the thoughts that went through my mind but I can remember how I felt. It was a mixture of unutterable joy and paralyzing fear; two powerful emotions that in some wild and inexplicable way sat comfortably side by side.

And that is how the second phase of our relationship ended. The third phase began almost straight away, in fact on the very next night. We met where we had left off beneath the tree but neither of us made any reference to any of the preceding events. It was almost as if we had known one another all of our lives. Even so there was something very odd about him that I couldn't quite grasp. For example he didn't have a name nor did he seem to have any understanding of what it meant to have a name, as though he had no sense of self. I told him mine and he seemed quite content to accept the name that I had chosen for him – Simon. Also when I started to tell him about the real world in which I lived he didn't have a clue as to what I was talking about. He knew no other world and yet he obviously hadn't grown up here in this place because it was as new to him as it was to me.

And so throughout the following days and weeks each time we met, we spent the duration of the dream exploring that strange land. In the main I did most of the talking as Simon listened; and he listened like someone driven, desperate to learn, determined not to miss a thing.

It was at this point in time that I told my mother about him and I remember vaguely including him in my playing; he became my imaginary friend. After her initial concern, my mother soon accepted that this was not anything to be worried about and left me to it.

On one occasion however an event took place that cast a dark shadow over our hitherto very pleasant times together. We had just rounded a stack of massive boulders by the side of the stream, when, to our amazement the image of a woman seated on a bench appeared out of thin air directly ahead of us in much the same way that a photograph develops on the paper in a photographer's tank of chemicals. She looked straight at us and raised her hand to beckon us. I looked at Simon and he looked at me and I could tell that he was not at all comfortable with the situation and to tell the truth neither was I. But we carried on walking without slowing our pace very much until we were just a few yards away. At this point we stopped suddenly and almost without realizing what we were doing we held hands. The identity of the women was then very clear – to me at least. Then before I could do or say anything she jumped up from her seat and lunged at us grabbing hold of me. Her eyes were ablaze and saliva sprayed from her mouth – she was like some rabid animal. With hardly a pause for breath she yelled and yelled at Simon.

"Go away…go away. Leave him alone…get away from him…get away!"

Poor Simon just stood there as I struggled to free myself from her cold, clammy grasp. Eventually I was able to break away. I staggered back to Simon, who seemed rooted to the spot, grabbed his arm and tried to drag him away. Keeping one eye on the woman I pulled and pulled on what felt like a huge block of stone.

"Come on," I screamed. "Come on Simon."

At last he seemed to respond; he snapped his head round to look at me and we set off running back the way we had come. We ran and ran and didn't stop until we were safely under the canopy of our tree and there we collapsed side by side gasping for breath.

As it happened time ran out for us before either of us could say anything about what had just occurred. Everything began to fade – the sign that the dream was coming to an end.

But then something happened in one of the dreams very soon after that incident that planted the thought in my mind that there was far more to this than mere dreams.

We met as usual and straight away he asked me two very disturbing questions. The first I had half expected referring back to the previous incident with the woman. It was the phrase he used to refer to her that made the hairs on the back of my neck stand on end. This is what he said. "Why did that woman… that mother person say such horrible things about me?"

I was dumb struck. I just stared at him. But then he dropped another bombshell without waiting for my reply.

"Oh, and another thing; when we separate...what happens to you?"

My jaw dropped even further. From his demeanour it was quite apparent that he was not so much anxious or troubled by these issues than interested in much the same way that he had always been since the very beginning. He sat down on a rock and looked at me expectantly. I recovered my composure but didn't answer straight away even though the answer to his second question at least was obvious. As for the first question I decided that I wouldn't even try to address it at this time.

I walked over to join him on the rock and as I turned the question over in my mind it struck me just how serious a point it raised. Had I imagined it or had he laid particular emphasis on the 'you'? I know all about me because I'm a real person but how on earth can Simon, this figment of my imagination in my dream, have any concept of 'other place'? That would infer that he too was a real person and that was simply too much to contemplate so I let the question hang there a little longer and then said casually and rather stupidly.

"Oh I just get up and get on with my day...why?"

"Mmm...just a thought. Don't know really."

The tone of his reply made it very clear that he was far from satisfied with my answer but I was desperate to move on. I couldn't face the twists and turns that would emerge if we had to follow that one, but as I suspected I wouldn't be able to avoid them for long and this is where the fourth and final phase began.

I can't be sure of when exactly, probably a day or two later, but we were ambling along, not saying very much, when Simon suddenly sat down and sprawled out on the grass.

"Let's have a rest," he said.

I thought it rather odd but went along with it. We lay in silence for some time before Simon spoke again and it was quite obvious from what he said that the question he had asked previously was still troubling him.

"I know you don't want to talk about it but let me tell you something and then I'll shut up."

"OK...go on," I replied. I owed him that, I suppose. He began hesitantly.

"When we are not together...when you're not here with me... I'm just... nowhere. I can't describe it any other way. It's like I'm in some...well just empty blackness...nothing to see nothing to hear. But I can still think and remember. It's weird."

Part of me wanted him to go on but the other part was frightened. The whole thing, which started off so innocently had, of recent times, begun to acquire some disturbing elements.

Then we did something we'd never done before and I can't easily say why we did it. It was as though the idea occurred to each of us at the same time and by mutual but unspoken consent we just did it. In silence we lay back in the grass. The stillness and warmth of the place had a soporific affect on me and I went to sleep, or at least that's what I assumed happened. Strange to think of it now – going off to sleep whilst already in a dream. Anyway what happened then convinced me that I no longer wished to continue our dream meetings. How I would accomplish that I had no idea.

In this strange sleep I felt myself sink into the earth, slowly, slowly, down into the ground. It's so difficult to describe what it felt like but it was as though I was passing into another dimension and the next moment I was floating; as far as I could tell just floating in an immense void. I could see, hear and feel nothing. But it wasn't space, well not space as I would have imagined it, it was more like being entombed in something solid but through which I could move.

Then in the distance a light appeared, just a tiny speck but it seemed to be approaching very quickly; apart from the fact that it was growing in size as it approached I could feel a shock wave ahead of it buffeting me through the strange medium. Seconds later the object was in front of me - a globe of brilliant light hovering not two feet away and about six feet in diameter. There was something going on inside the globe but I couldn't make out exactly what it was. But then as I gazed into it the scene became crystal clear. There within that sphere I saw two boys walking by a stream, skipping and laughing as they went. I knew straight away who they were but with the realization came a great weight of sadness. It was the sadness of loss and hopelessness-of deep tragedy. If I thought that was strange, the way I spoke to myself in my mind was even stranger because as I watched the two boys I was saying to myself things like 'Oh yeah I remember, it's me and Gordon playing...ha, ha, ha, yeah and then we tried to jump across the stream and Gordon fell in...he was wet through.' and 'It's me and Gordon having a race. He won again ...but I nearly beat him that time. Just you wait I'll be the winner soon.' But at the same time another part of me was shouting. "But I'm Gordon!! This doesn't make any sense. I'm talking as though I'm Simon"

To say that I was confused would be a great understatement. Thankfully it was not long before the globe of light began to fade and I felt myself returning; not though to my bed in the real world but back to the place where this began, next to Simon lying on the grass

I lay still and quiet for some time, not knowing whether Simon was asleep or awake. At last, out of curiosity I turned to see what he was doing. He was lying close to me, presumably in the same place as when we started, but his eyes were open and staring straight upwards. He didn't move at all when I turned my head to look at him and I must admit that, for one brief moment of panic, the thought went through my head that he may be dead. I sat up quickly to take a closer look and it was then that I noticed the tears. He had obviously been crying for some time as there were dry tear tracks across his cheeks as well as fresh rivulets that had formed puddles in his ears and in the earth beneath his head. I'd never seen anyone looking so utterly miserable. He mustn't have seen me or he just didn't care because the tears continued to well up and pour down his face for some time.

I never did get to the bottom of it because as I waited, expecting all the time that sooner or later he would come round, the scene began to fade; a sure sign that I was waking up.

"Come on Gordon...breakfast."

And that was it. I couldn't begin to imagine what had happened that had had such a profound effect on him as I was staring into that globe. Whatever it was must have been very significant for him as it was the last time we met for a long time. As I think about it, this in itself could be telling. Is it possible that somehow he was able to control whether or not we meet?

As the days turned into weeks and the months into years I reached a point where the whole thing was nothing but a dim and distant memory. But this, as I was soon to discover produced in me a very false sense of security.

Chapter 3

By the time I was fifteen, unlike most of my peers, I knew what I wanted to do with my life. I had always had a strong leaning towards sciences and more recently this had crystallized more specifically into a desire to become a doctor. In all areas my life was as settled as could reasonably be expected in someone of my age and the strange events of earlier years were now nothing more than entries in the scrap book of my mind.

But then, over a period of just a few weeks I became increasingly aware of his presence; no longer in my dreams but in real time and I can't deny that it was a scary feeling. The first thing that crossed my mind was that I was going a bit loopy. I'd dabbled a bit with pot, smoked a few joints when I'd been out with my friends and I'd heard that cannabis had been implicated in the onset of schizophrenia in young adults. I got so scared at one point that I thought of going to my own doctor but I decided to read up about it first. That went some way towards allaying my fear because I didn't have any symptoms of social withdrawal or lack of motivation and I certainly didn't feel that my actions were under the control of someone else; it was just the vague feeling that he, Simon, was there, wherever 'there' was. It manifested itself in odd ways like if I'd decided to go somewhere at the weekend with my friends another 'suggestion' would come into my mind to do something quite different. I use the word 'suggestion' intentionally because that was what it seemed to be, not simply an alternative idea that came from my own mind.

The crunch came one evening as I was sitting at my desk in my bedroom preparing to do some homework. As clear as day I heard these words just as if spoken by someone directly behind me.

"Hello   Gordon…   Gordon…   It's me…me…Simon."

I spun round to see who was there, but there was no one. The words on the page of the book in front of me blurred and for those few moments I was close to blind panic. I swallowed hard and took several deep breaths, talking to myself all the time.

'C'mon Gordon…get a grip of yourself. You're imagining things. Sleep, that's what you need…a good night's sleep.'

"No… you're not… imagining anything. But I'm finding it… hard to do… this… be in touch…can't…can't quite…"

It stopped as abruptly as it started. Just like the transmission of a weak radio signal breaking up with adverse atmospheric conditions. Nevertheless there was no mistaking it and my heart lurched. I remained speechless at my desk for a good fifteen minutes, dreading a recurrence of the voice. When it seemed there was to be none, I rose from my chair, steadying myself against the desk, slowly and shakily undressed and slid into bed. Needless to say I did not drift effortlessly off to sleep that night but when it did come it was filled with very strange and disturbing dreams. Not the dreams of our meetings, although there was very clear reference to them; rather it was a bizarre mixture of that world, filled with illuminated globes bouncing around all over the place, and the real world in which I was in my back garden looking into the house but as if I was Simon and my parents were seated at the dining table eating lunch together. I was terrified but despite my yelling and screaming no one paid any attention to me. This last bit of the dream occurred over and over again and each time my distress grew more and more intense until I was hammering on the window with blooded fists. I awoke yelling into my pillow and beating the mattress like someone demented. I flung myself out of bed and just stood there shaking, staring. My bedside clock said 5.30. I went to the window, drew back the curtains and looked out onto a grey dawn waiting for the comfortable ordinariness of it to soothe the turmoil within. The cold glass on my forehead and a sudden shaft of sunlight bursting through a chink in the cloud just above the horizon sent a tingle through my aching body. I looked up at the gradually brightening sky, stretched and took a deep breath, letting it out very slowly. This seemed to do the trick – the demon was evaporating like mist on a summer morning and soon I felt able get on with the day.

For the next hour or so I tackled the homework from which I had been disturbed, had a shower and went downstairs for breakfast. Despite the odd occasion when I experienced what I can only describe as a vague presence there was no recurrence of anything quite so disturbing as before.

All of this took place just a few weeks before my 'O' levels began. These went pretty much according to plan and the end result was a very satisfactory set of grades-enough, at any rate, to get me into the sixth form studying the sciences I needed. Much to my great delight there were no further occurrences of previous events during the whole of my first year sixth form, in fact not until the spring term of my upper sixth did anything of any note take place. Then two very significant things happened, one very, very good and one extremely bad. The good came in the shape of Katy and the other...

It was one Thursday lunchtime and I was with a group of friends in the queue at the refectory.

"Eh, eh, you lot just take a gander over there. No you daft sod over there." said Keith pointing towards a table in the corner near the drinks machine.

Danny and I saw her straight away. We just stood there gawping but the others seemed more interested in what was on the menu and we were soon pushed along by the weight of hungry students eager to fill their bellies.

"Bloody hell she's a cracker. Who is she?" asked Danny, still unable to take his eyes off her and saying yes to whatever was being offered to him by the serving staff.

"I've seen her before…don't know her name," I said. "But I'm going to find out," I added quietly, more to myself than anyone else.

We sat down at a strategically placed table and ate our lunch amid much ribald commentary aimed, as you would expect, at the vision that had captured our attention. After about ten minutes she got up to leave. At our table all mouths ceased chewing, all jaws dropped and all eyes followed her as she returned her tray to the collection point and left the refectory. Only then did the banter and the eating resume.

"She's gorgeous…absolutely gorgeous," drooled Danny. "I bet you don't even say hello never mind anything else," he continued, jabbing his knife at me.

"You're on pal," I replied. "In fact I bet you, I'll go out with her too…aye…this weekend," I added defiantly but thinking that perhaps I'd gone too far.

The others laughed and clapped but it only served to increase my determination to do as I had said or at least give it a go.

Early that same afternoon I found myself with a free half hour and decided to go for a coffee. It would be rather pretentious to call it a coffee bar as it was nothing more than a partitioned off part of what was once the assembly hall of the original grammar school. The old herringbone parquet floor had been covered with a pale green washable linoleum type material, with some easy chairs and low tables scattered around. Several vending machines were dotted about the place and the overall effect was appropriately one of casual comfort and serviceability.

I went to the nearest machine and placed my money in the slot. As I waited for the clicking and whirring to finish I glanced around the room looking for someone with whom to sit. Even from behind and slouched down in the chair she was unmistakable. I couldn't believe my luck. But the bravado with which I had at first declared my intent turned out to be just that, now that I was not in the company of my friends. I was on the point of taking my drink and sneaking away to the furthest corner of the room when she turned round and looked in my direction.

Despite giving the appearance of looking straight at me it was obvious from the rather vacant expression on her face that she could not in fact see me at all clearly. Then she looked down and seemed to be fumbling with something on her lap. Eventually she put a pair of neat glasses on and looked again towards me. Her face lit up with a smile and she beckoned me over with a wave of her hand. I looked around to see if there was someone else at whom she was directing her attention but I was alone. Taking my drink and with pounding heart I walked towards her watching her all the time as she cleared a space on the table in front of her. She had dark, shoulder length wavy hair which tumbled over her face each time she bent forward or leaned to one side and, despite constantly being brushed back into place there always seemed to be a few determined strands that hung around her eyes and face thereby lending an overall dishevelled yet even more alluring look to her. Finally it would seem, irritated beyond endurance, she scraped it all back and held it in place with a wide emerald green band. As I got nearer my nerve began to fail me and by the time I was across the table from her I was so unsteady that I missed the seat as I went to sit down and ended up on the floor with half the contents of my cup all over me.

"Oops, careful," she giggled. "Or you'll have none left…here give it me."

She took the cup from me and placed it on the table. By this time I was as red as a beetroot having been ignominiously abandoned by the ultra cool persona who had been, up to this point, just about managing to hold his own

"Oh hell…I'm so sorry," I blurted "I'm not usually such a clumsy sod."

"That's OK…do you want to get yourself another drink?" she said, indicating with a nod the mess on the floor and smiling. "You've not much left."

There was something about her look and the way she said it that had us both in fits of laughter that echoed around the near empty hall.

"Well that's one way of getting to know someone," she said, dabbing her eyes with a tissue and trying not to start laughing again.

"Aye…works every time... all part of the plan," I said, feeling some return of dignity.

"Well I don't believe that for a start," she replied.

"Step number two… names. I'm…" I began.

"Gordon, yeah I know," she interrupted and then looked a little embarrassed.

'Mmm,' I thought, 'now why would she know that?' My heart leapt at the thought that perhaps she'd had her eye on me but then I told myself not to be so stupid.

"Well you've got one over on me because I don't know yours."

"It's Katy…with a Y…not a how or a when but a Y," she smiled, raising her eyebrows playfully.

floor...and of course that gorgeous bird back there. More often than not I can't see anything, but I'm working on that one. I can hear you...most of the time anyway."

"Oh my God. Oh my God. What's happening to me?"

"Stop saying that you pillock. Look I don't know any more than you do about how, but here we are and...anyway...just to let you know...I'm here. You've had a bit of a shock...and d'you know, I can feel that too? This is getting very interesting but I'll be off for now. Catch you soon."

And he was gone - just like that. The acute sense of panic and bewilderment began to fade. I can't say that I felt OK again because I didn't but I felt some control returning. I stayed slumped against the tree for a little longer until I'd stopped shaking and then continued albeit unsteadily homewards. Once back home, with the reassurance and comfort of the familiar, I soon began to feel much better especially as my mind turned to Katy. I needed to check the cinema listing and call her. First I needed to get rid of my school stuff which I promptly did up in my bedroom. Back downstairs for a piece of toast and a glass of milk; then a look at the cinema listing in the paper.

'Mmm not much to my taste,' I thought. 'Still I'll let Katy choose,' and with that I went to phone her. After several false starts I eventually picked up the receiver and dialled.

"Hello."

"Oh hi Katy. It's me."

"Which 'me' is it…there's so many?"

"Me…Gordon."

"Oh that me. Hi Gordon."

"You're not fair you know," I said.

"Oh?"

"You've no idea how many times I've started to phone you and bottled it at the last minute."

"Oh I'm sorry Gordon…go on, what've you found for us to see."

Her voice bubbled with mischievous glee each time she spoke and my heart just went crazy. I told her what was on and she agreed that there wasn't much to choose from so we agreed to meet in town and just go for a drink. I put the phone down and went back up to my room.

"There that wasn't so bad Gordon was it?"

My stomach hit the floor once again. This time though I sat on the edge of my bed shut my eyes and took several deep breaths. I decided that it was no use denying that there was something in this – that it wasn't my imagination – that I wasn't going mad and that I had to face it and deal with it somehow.

"Simon…it is you isn't it?" I felt rather foolish as I spoke into the empty room but I couldn't afford to stay on the back foot.

"Of course it's me."

"Mmm."

"What do you mean, 'Mmm'?" he said.

"Well look, neither of us can understand this…this…whatever is happening but you can't just keep dropping in on me like this…you know it's…well it's crazy."

Even as I was speaking I felt my mind flip this way and that way as I struggled to accept that this was really happening.

"I must be going mad!" I shouted finally to the empty room.

There was an immediate and emphatic response that I could not deny as coming from somewhere else. Sure it was in my mind, and I suppose anyone being privy to my experience would say that I was hallucinating but I was utterly convinced that this was not the case.

"Gordon you are not hallucinating," he said most emphatically. "I am here…I really am. I can tell you about our dreams, about the places we used to visit…d'you remember in the early days that bloody woman, your mother dragging you away from me?"

"Yeah 'course, why?"

"Well just listen to this. I knew I'd have to tell you this sometime and now…well just hear me out."

He didn't speak straight away; I sensed his reticence.

"Go on," I said. "Go on Simon," I repeated softly.

"There's been a few times now...not when we've met in dreams... when I've been on my own..."

He paused again.

"Oh it's so hard to put into words. It's as though I get into your world...your real world, whatever that is. I kind of wake up in your body and see what you see but I can't do anything by myself...I've no control. And then just as quickly it's gone and I'm back in my world."

I sensed he was becoming agitated and a great sense of sadness flooded through me which I struggled to understand. It was as if the sadness wasn't mine.

"Simon...what's wrong?"

Tears welled up in my eyes and I had no idea why.

"Oh God Gordon you have no idea what my world is like. Emptiness...just absolute total... nothingness. And since I've come to know your world it makes it even worse. It's like living in hell and every now and then I get a glimpse of heaven... but I know that I always have to go back to that empty bleak world that is...well... hell."

"I do know something of what it's like in your world y'know. When we lay down side by side...you remember ages ago? We must have changed places for a while and I saw things...weird things that must be your world...but anyway go on. Tell me what you wanted to say; something about going into my world. What did you see?"

Simon was quiet for a while but his presence was so intense that it was almost suffocating- as though he was battling to occupy the same space as myself. Then he began telling me such a tale that I was barely aware of breathing.

"I found myself in a room. It was a large room with great big windows at one end looking out onto a long garden. There was a dark green leather suite and a small polished wood table in the main part and a glass cabinet on the same wall as the television."

He went on in great detail to describe my house. Then to tell me about how my mother, that mother as he called her, came in with a cup of tea and sat down to read the newspaper. Then he/I came into the room, said "Hi Mum," and went into the kitchen. Then my dad came in from the garden and asked had anyone seen his new hoe? It seemed to go on for ages, describing all the rooms in the house, the food in our cupboards, and the stuff in my bedroom; and then he stopped abruptly.

"And then it all began to fade and I was lying next to you. Oh God I was so disappointed that I had to leave. It was beautiful. I'd have given anything to have stayed."

I was stunned. I hardly knew what to think. But that was obviously why he was crying.

"So…you've…you know what it's like in my house. You've seen me and my mum and dad at home. Did no one say anything when you...?"

I realised it was a stupid question almost as soon as I began to ask and he cut in angrily.

"Well of course not idiot, 'cos I wasn't actually there was I…I must have just tapped in to your mind…just like I'm doing now. And kind of...well... seen your memories or something…oh I don't know."

"So where do we go from here?"

"I've no idea," he replied.

He sounded as exhausted as I felt.

"Anyway I'm knackered," I said at last. "I'm knackered and confused...I haven't a bloody clue what's going on and I can't begin to guess what's going to happen, so..."

There was nothing else to say. As I lay on my bed I sensed that he was moving away. Neither of us said another word and I reckon that within a couple of minutes he'd gone and I'd fallen asleep.

Chapter 4

The following day I woke at 6.30 feeling surprisingly good considering all that had happened the previous evening, and it was with that new-day energy that I got ready for school. I had a quick breakfast, exchanging a few words with my mum, left the house and took the path through the forest once again. There had always been something special about that journey, except when it was pouring down and I was late, but that morning it was particularly wonderful. I put it down to the fact that it was Friday, I was going to see Katy and we were arranging our evening out. 'Fantastic' I said to myself and laughed out loud, adding to the raucous exuberance of the rooks high up in the trees. It was going to be a great day.

The day went well. Katy and I arranged to meet by the statues in the town centre at seven. And I gloated all day in the company of my friends who couldn't believe it when I told them that I was seeing her. Danny and I walked some of the way home together and parted at the bridge that passed over the river where we had often played in our younger days.

"Don't forget now, I want a blow by blow account of how you get on tonight," he shouted as he crossed the bridge. "You jammy sod," he added loudly, shaking his head,

"Aye OK...see you," I replied, but with no intention of telling anybody anything at all.

Once back home, I made myself a sandwich and went to my room to eat it at my desk. Afterwards, I had a shower and lounged around in my dressing gown downstairs, flicking through the TV channels; at which point my mother came in. We chatted a while. I told her a little bit about Katy and then went to get ready to go out. Dad was just arriving home as I was leaving.

"Oh hello...and goodbye," he said delivering a mock punch to my stomach as we almost clashed in the hall.

"See you later...Mum'll fill you in, no doubt, about my forthcoming night of drunken debauchery."

"What?" he exclaimed to my retreating figure.

"Nothing...see you." I shouted. I set off at a run in order not to miss the bus I needed to get me to town on time.

I saw her before she saw me. She was seated on a bench beneath the plinth of one of the two statues that flanked the town hall steps. I decided to creep up on her from behind but just as I was about to grab her she jumped to her feet, stood on the bench and launched herself at me, almost knocking me to the ground. I'd never met anyone like her before – though to be honest I'd not had much experience with girls at all. The odd one or two when I was fifteen or sixteen; you know it lasts for a few days and has its fair share of snogging and groping, but that's all. This was in a different league. She was fun, interesting and of course gorgeous - and I think she liked me.

"You're mad, d'you know that?" I said taking her hand.

She looked up at me and said seriously.

"You're not the first who's said that...funny ...mmm perhaps it's true," she added frowning slightly.

"I think I nearly believe you. Anyway let's get that drink."

The thing is I'd only been in to a pub three or four times and I was concerned not to make a fool of myself. To be honest I didn't much like beer but it just seemed to be the thing to drink, 'it's a man thing.' Some older friends had said that they felt just the same when they started and that in time you get to like it. A rite of passage I suppose.

We crossed the square and headed for the Blue Boar. It was the only pub I'd been to in the town centre so at least I felt a little more confident. Katy slipped her hand into mine and I felt a million dollars. As we walked and chatted I took every opportunity to look at her. She was about three inches shorter than me, with a very trim figure – petite is probably the best way to describe her. Her hair was dark and lustrous; I could imagine running my fingers through it and watching it tumble over her face just as it had done when I first met her. She wasn't wearing her glasses which gave me an opportunity to look at her eyes properly. Rich brown irises flecked with black and set against the blue tinged whites – stunningly beautiful. Her lashes were so thick that it looked as if her eyes were bordered by a soft haze and as for her eyebrows; they too were very dark and neatly shaped to flick upwards at the ends. 'Mmm' I thought, 'very cat-like…fits perfectly with her mane of hair. I bet she's got claws as well.' At this point my imagination took rather a lurid turn and I had to reign myself in. Her nose was clearly defined, slender with nostrils that flared as she spoke, but the most alluring feature, after her eyes, was her mouth. Her full lips, with corners which turned upwards slightly, never quite met in the middle so always revealing a sliver of pure white teeth. When she spoke her whole face became animated as she expressed joy or disgust or anger over something. I could hardly take my eyes off her and more than once came near to colliding with a lamppost as we walked along.

It was a warm evening and if I'd thought about it a bit more I'd have suggested going out of the town for a drink, but it was too late to do anything about it.

The old sign bearing a now much faded painting of a blue wild boar swung lazily in the evening breeze. I pushed the heavy door and we made our way into the gloomy interior where it was quite apparent that not much had changed in the last fifty years. Even though it was early evening and there was hardly anyone in, we were met by a none-too-pleasant waft of almost foetid air – heavy with the smell of stale beer and smoke.

"Oh God," I said as much to myself as to Katy. It hadn't registered before what a dump it was, but then when you're out with your mates you don't notice such things as decor and smells.

"Mmm, it is a bit isn't? Never mind let's sit over there by that open window...at least we'll get some fresh air."

Katy picked her way between the heavy iron tables and sat on the bench seat by the window as I went to get the drinks. When I returned she'd removed her jacket and had shifted to one of the more comfortable looking armchairs on the adjoining table. She sat back, with one elbow on the chair arm and her head cradled in her cupped hand; just watching me and smiling.

"What's amusing you?" I asked, placing the drinks down on the table.

"Nothing...why?" she replied.

"Oh...just..."

"Just what?"

"You look like you're...weighing me up," I said, taking a drink.

"Well, what if I am…I quite like what I see. Is that OK?"

I must admit I was taken aback by her directness, but thrilled to bits at the same time. For a moment or two I really didn't know how to respond.

"Well in that case, just a minute."

I then proceeded to look her up and down in a much exaggerated manner as though evaluating her at an auction.

"Mmm…you know what? I like what I see too…very much do I like it."

We looked at one another in silence for a few seconds and then, maybe out of embarrassment at the realization of some shared unspoken intimacy, we each picked up our glasses and took a drink.

We talked about all kinds of things for the next hour or so until it began to get crowded and uncomfortably smoky at which point we agreed to leave.

It was almost dark as we ambled back across town. We weren't heading anywhere in particular, simply enjoying the fresh air, the quiet streets and the opportunity to chat and hold hands. The fountains outside the town hall had been switched off for the day and a few cheeky sparrows were scavenging among the rubbish that lay in the bottom of the now dry basin. Here and there squabbling pigeons were laying claim to their roost for the night on ledges and window-sills above the shops. Apart from a few couples like us and the odd group of rowdy young men making their way from one bar to another we had the place to ourselves. Give it another couple of hours and it would be very different as the cinemas and theatres emptied and the pubs close. So we had a little time to enjoy the solitude

"So what've you got on this weekend?" Katy asked.

"Well, apart from getting some studying done, I was hoping that we could go out somewhere...perhaps a walk tomorrow," I replied.

"Sounds good. Where to?"

"Oh I dunno. Maybe get a bus out to Brandlewood and walk across to Egglinton. I know a good route...it's a bit rough in places but we'd manage. What d'you say?"

"Ok I'll bring a picnic."

"Brilliant...I'll bring some bits too. Is 11 o'clock OK? I'll meet you at your stop."

"Mmm, I'll look forward to that."

The Town Hall clock had just struck ten. Two minutes later we turned into the bus station and made our way to her stop. As we stood under the shelter she snuggled up close and put her head against my shoulder. We didn't speak much, there didn't seem any need. Then as the driver started the engine and opened the doors, she looked up at me, gave me a kiss full on the mouth and then jumped aboard. I must have looked like an idiot, standing there with a silly smile on my face. As the bus pulled away she blew me a kiss and went to sit down. She looked out of the window at me and gestured that I should give her a ring. I walked to the other side of the bus station and boarded my bus which was just about to leave. I spent the whole journey going over the events of the evening, savouring each wonderful memory. Lost in thought as I was, it was a tremendous shock when Simon burst into my head.

"What a fantastic night eh? Didn't catch all of it… I've not mastered it yet but I will in time."

"What...what d'you mean?" I yelled.

The other passenger looked round in alarm but I didn't care.

"What the bloody hell d'you mean by that?" I cried again, this time under my breath through clenched teeth. I was fuming mad. "Stop this Simon...you can't keep doing this. You're...you're being a bloody pain in the neck."

"I'm being a pain am I? I'm a pest am I? You just wait...I haven't even begun yet. I know how to get through now and nothing's going to stop me...it's my turn Gordon, d'you hear? My turn and you can't stop me."

For the first time since we came face to face so to speak I was frightened. I didn't understand how any of this could be happening but I was very frightened. It felt like he was gaining control and that I was losing it. I had to do something. But then it occurred to me that he could only reach me in my head, he didn't actually have any means of doing anything. All I had to do was keep a cool head and resist him.

"Right Simon," I began defiantly, "You and I both know that you can't really do anything. You are just a noise and a bloody annoying one at that so just go and piss off."

His reply was instant and threatening.

"You're right Gordon...for the time being, but I'm learning all the time and I'm telling you, the time will come when I'll be in control. That's not a threat Gordon it's a promise. Just think on this. You experience my feelings just as much as I do yours and I detect fear in you. You see I have nothing to lose."

"Oh yeah, yeah, yeah," I said defiantly as I left my seat and made my way to the front of the bus. "Just go and stuff yourself Simon...you can do nothing. You're all blather."

I resolved to have no further exchanges with Simon – not then at least and whether he understood that or not I don't know but he remained silent for the rest of the night. The cool night air felt good as I walked the few hundred yards to my house. It gave me breathing space; time to shake off the effects of our unpleasant exchange and to get it into perspective. I reiterated what I had said to Gordon, as much for my sake I suppose. He didn't have any power to control me; he was just bluffing, trying his hand. Even so there was maybe one percent of my mind that harboured a doubt, the tiniest of fears.

There was something good and reassuring about the short walk up the path to the front door. I stood for a few moments looking in through the window. Mum and dad were sitting watching TV just as they've done on weekend nights for as long as I can remember. I used to sit with them just a few short years ago and have a mug of Horlicks before going to bed. I didn't think much of it then but standing there looking in, it brought back such warm feelings of comfort and security. Here I am now, too old for such things and can't go back; though at that moment I'd have given anything just to curl up again between my mum and dad and drink my Horlicks. It made me feel quite sad, but that's life, as they say; everything moves on. I moved on and in through the front door.

"Hi Gordon...d'you have a good time?" shouted my mother.

I went into the lounge and sat in an armchair. Mum smiled and asked again.

"So was it good...your film?"

"Oh we decided not to go in the end...mostly rubbish so we just walked around."

"And went to the pub?" dad interjected without taking his eyes off the TV.

"Who, me?" I exclaimed, feigning indignation.

"Yes you…I have my spies. Let me see now…er how about "The Commercial"?"

"Blue Boar actually…didn't stay long. Too smoky…it's horrible. Anyway I'm off to bed. See you tomorrow."

"Yeah OK…just in time for lunch as usual?" said my mum teasingly.

"Not tomorrow," I said. "I need to be up early…we're having a picnic."

"Picnic…we? Oh yes…I remember… Katy isn't it?" said mum.

"Aye that's right."

Then before anyone could say another word I disappeared upstairs.

I could hardly wait for the following day and felt sure that I would be unable to sleep. As for the argument with Simon earlier, I had dealt with that and was confident that he would cause no further problem-at least not that night.

When I slept though, I had a most disturbing dream. It was unlike anything I'd had before. The great oak tree was the main feature but it was nowhere near as big as in previous dreams. I was under the canopy and Simon stood just outside of it facing me. I was panic stricken and terrified, trying desperately to escape from under it but each time I stepped with one foot outside Simon pushed me back and slammed a door in my face. I worked my way all around the perimeter looking for a way out but he kept pushing me back and closing the doors until I was in complete darkness. I could hear him on the outside and I could tell that he was walking away. All he said as he went was, "Goodbye Gordon, good-bye...enjoy being me."

I woke up shaking, my bedclothes wet with sweat. I reached out with a trembling hand and switched on my bedside light. It was only 5.30 but I knew I wouldn't be able to get back to sleep. I tried to read but to no avail and by the time it was seven o'clock I gave up and went downstairs for a glass of milk. I mooched around in my room for the next hour or so rummaging aimlessly through the contents of my desk drawers and my books until I felt it was time to get ready.

The sunlight, an invigorating shower and the sound of birdsong soon dispelled the after effects of the dream and by 9 o'clock I was packed and ready. I still had plenty of time so I sat at my desk with a view to organising some of my A level notes. As I was flicking through my Biology text book it opened wide at a page on which there was a large diagram of a pregnant uterus. I had seen this before many times but this time there was something most disturbing about it; in some strange way it reminded me of the dream I'd just had. It was quite scary. I couldn't rid myself of the thought of being trapped for ever inside the uterus, never to be born. I struggled to catch my breath as Simon's words went round and round in my head. "Now it's my turn...now it's my turn." Once again I felt the rising panic. I jumped from the desk and went to the window. Flinging it wide open I stuck my head out and breathed deeply. Immediately beneath me my mother was hanging out some washing and the sound of the window banging above must have startled her.

"Oh my goodness what was that?" she exclaimed, dropping two of the pegs that she was holding in her mouth. Then, looking up and seeing me fully dressed, "Blimey, fancy seeing you up at this time on a Saturday morning...she must be a bit special," she added, bending down to retrieve the dropped pegs.

"Hi mum...sorry...didn't mean to make you jump. See you in a sec," I said as I quickly withdrew my head and closed the window again.

I turned and leaned with my back against the wall for a few moments drinking in the ordinariness of what had just happened – my mother pegging out, the garden bursting with life, birdsong, the sky and warm sunshine – and allowing it to dispel the darkness that had threatened to overwhelm me again.

I went to my desk and slammed shut the textbook without looking at the picture; then collected a small rucksack and my jacket from the wardrobe and left my room. I hurriedly downed a bowl of cereal, shouted my goodbyes to whoever could hear and left the house. As I had plenty of time and as it was a beautiful day I decided to walk the two miles or so into town. On the way I stopped to buy a few packets of crisps, some cans of coke and a couple of chocolate bars.

The walk did me good. It cleared my head wonderfully and with ten minutes to spare I sat across from Katy's bus stop, opened a pack of crisps and waited for her.

Chapter 5

My heart began to thump as her bus turned into the station and came to a halt. I watched eagerly as the passengers alighted until at last I saw her. She looked around and, on seeing me, waved and ran across to me. I took her hands in mine and kissed her on the cheek. She in turn withdrew her hands from mine, took my face between them and kissed me gently on the lips.

"Hi," she said smiling as she pulled away.

"Hi to you," I replied, weak-kneed and then adding after a few seconds pause to catch my breath, "are you all set?"

"Ready for anything."

"C'mon then."

We got to the stop just as the bus was about to pull away, paid and went upstairs. The air was stuffily warm and damp, but thankfully had not yet built up the acrid fug of stale cigarette smoke that would develop as the day wore on. The bus trundled slowly along the Saturday-morning, crowd-thronged streets of the town centre, gradually making its way out northwards. The large office blocks and stores were soon left behind to be replaced by small business premises, and eventually street after street of old terraced houses. Here and there scattered amongst this warren of streets there stood an old mill. These were the monolithic testaments to the success and unimaginable wealth of the few, and once the place of employment of the multitude - at least one occupant from every single house around. They were all that was left of the dozens of mills that dominated the industry of this and towns like it in this part of England during the nineteenth and early twentieth century.

"It's funny isn't it?" Katy said pensively, "How different things look from the top of a bus. You can see into people's backyards and gardens…sometimes even into their bedrooms…loads of things you'd never see otherwise. It's like looking into their lives in some way."

"Mmm…I know what you mean," I agreed. But I wasn't looking out; I was watching her. The way her hair shone with rich copper hues as the sun caught it. The way her lips parted and pouted ever so slightly as her tongue ran over them, leaving them moist and glistening. The way her soft dark eyes flitted back and forth as each thing that caught her interest passed and was left behind only to be replaced by the next. I would have been happy to spend the whole day just driving round and round if I could have watched her like that all the time. Occasionally she would turn to me and smile and then return to her watching; it was wonderful.

Gradually the scenery changed from urban to semi-rural to rural. From that point very few people got on or off the bus. Up to the left lay open moorland and to the right, farming pasture sweeping away into a wide shallow valley. We spoke little for most of the journey; it was enough just to hold hands and exchange glances and smiles now and then. At last we rounded a bend in the road and I recognised just ahead the restaurant that I'd visited with my mum and dad on several occasions.

"C'mon this is our stop," I said taking Katy's hand and pressing the bell.

We stood on the grass verge and watched the bus as it chugged away amid a cloud of diesel fumes. Fifty yards further on it turned sharp left and disappeared behind a tall hawthorn hedge.

"Right, Mr Expedition leader, where are we off to?" cried Katy, turning her collar up because although it was warm there was a cool wind coming off the moors.

"Over there, Miss Katy," I said, pointing across a field to our right in the direction of some farm buildings. "It's a proper footpath...I've been before."

We climbed a stile over the wall and set off. The ground was baked hard making it difficult to walk in places because of the ruts and ridges that did not give when stood on. We picked our way across the first field, over another style and on past the farm.

We walked for about half an hour or so and I was beginning to feel a little hungry.

"What've you got to eat?" I asked.

"Sandwiches…ham I think."

"You think? Did you not make them?" I asked accusingly.

"No my mum did. Why, what have you got?'

"Crisps, chocolate and coke."

"Oh well you've really put yourself out haven't you?" she said digging me in the ribs. "You've no room to talk."

"Suppose so…anyway do you fancy stopping for a bit. I'm peckish?"

"Mmm, me too. What about that place over there?" she said pointing to what looked like an old barn. It had clouded over and was looking like it could rain.

"Good idea. C'mon I'll race you," I shouted setting off at a run.

"Oi…cheat…that's not fair"' she called.

But she need not have worried because after ten paces or so I was sprawling on my stomach having stepped awkwardly into a particularly deeply rutted patch of ground. I was in agony. When Katy caught me up she thought I was joking and stood over me laughing.

"I'm not joking Katy honest…here give us a hand up."

With a bit of help and support I managed to stand and slowly, with my arm around her shoulder we made our way to the barn.

The main doors were padlocked shut but we found a small side door that had not been securely fastened. Using a hefty piece of old gate post we prised it open and squeezed through. Inside it was dry and out of the wind. The old flag roof was in a bad state of repair allowing spears of light to strike through the dust laden air. At one end there was a stack of straw bales piled ten, maybe fifteen feet high and at the other end there were some sheep pens roughly made out of broken pallets and odd bits of timber tied together with baling twine.

"This'll do fine for a while," she said looking round. "I'll make a bit of a bench so you can lie on it and put your foot up…needs to be raised you know."

"Yeah I know…helps reduce swelling."

"Yeah. Just sit there for a minute," she added, pointing to an upturned bucket.

She dragged some of the bales into place and then helped me onto them before flopping down beside me.

"We can't hang around for too long Katy."

"I know but just an hour…it'll give any swelling a chance to go down. And besides we've not eaten yet, c'mon lets break out the banquet."

Granted it wasn't the Ritz but just being there together, eating our sandwiches and crisps, was fantastic. And afterwards all I wanted to do was to hold her in my arms but I didn't have the guts.

Imagine my surprise then when she got up from where she was seated across from me and came to sit next to me; and not just next to me but in such a way that she could bend forward and bring her face close to mine. Now imagine how I felt when she placed her lips next to mine and kissed me – not tenderly but hungrily; imagine how I felt when she lay down beside me and then on top of me, all the time kissing, kissing. For a moment she lifted her face away from me giving me the chance to unzip her jacket. Underneath she was wearing a dark blue polo neck sweater. Her hair tumbled over us wildly and I ached to crush her to me once again. Thrusting my hands under her sweater my heart skipped another beat as I felt her warm flesh and our lips met once more. But then it became too much for me – the feel of her breasts against my chest and her legs entwining mine; I could do nothing to stop it. And as the ecstasy faded I was overcome with such embarrassment I didn't know where to look. Katy of course knew exactly what had happened, but she didn't move away as I thought she would. Instead she just kissed me softly and said.

"It's OK Gordon…honestly. I shouldn't have been so…well…you know."

"Oh Katy," I said, lifting her head away so that I could see her more clearly, "I feel such an idiot."

She leant forward again to kiss me lightly and said simply. "Sshh…c'mon…go and get sorted out."

"But…it's not a problem I've ever had before," I said and then thought that perhaps that was not the best way to say what I meant. "No…I mean…I…it's not something I…I mean."

"Gordon," she said softly. "I know what you mean…just go and sort yourself out…here take these."

She handed me a small pack of tissues.

"Go on…I'll wait here…and try not to laugh, she continued, hardly managing to stifle a giggle. "Men… they're so untidy," she said more to her-self this time.

When I came back Katy had packed up the remnants of our picnic and had fashioned a makeshift walking stick for me. I was still feeling acutely embarrassed and found it difficult to look at her. She must have realised this because the next moment she placed her hands on my shoul-ders, turned me to face her and kissed me ten-derly on the lips.

"Honestly it's fine…It was as much my fault. Don't give it another thought. I've enjoyed today very much…c'mon don't let this little thing spoil it."

I threw my arms around her and squeezed her tight.

"Let's go…here take this." she said offering me the stick.

We forced our way through the doorway again and walked slowly along the path that led ultimately to the small village of Egglinton from where, after a half hour wait we caught a bus back home.

When we arrived back at the bus station it was still only five o'clock so we decided to go for a coffee before going home. A table for two looking out onto the town hall square gave us a good vantage point from which to watch late shoppers.

"Isn't it interesting just watching people?" she said gazing out of the window.

"Mmm…there are some funny folk aren't there?" I commented as a couple walked past, he being on the receiving end of a good tongue lashing from his diminutive partner.

"Oh you're not kidding…and look at her over there," she said pointing to a young woman who was struggling to stay upright.

"Drunk as a skunk at this time of day; what a mess," I added.

"Anyway, enough of that. What are you doing tomorrow?" Katy asked turning her attention to me.

"Nothing planned in particular, why?" I said, curious.

"Well my folks are away for the day…going to visit my uncle, my dad's brother, in Newcastle. He's not been too well, and I wondered if you fancied coming over…I'll cook us a meal."

Katy didn't lift her eyes from her cup as she spoke these words and my heart skipped more than a beat or two. I didn't need to be asked again.

"Honestly? That sounds fantastic…but will it be OK…you know with your folks?"

She looked up straight at me and smiled.

"Oh sure…no problem at all," she said. "Curry OK?"

"Magic," I said. "What time...oh and where do you live?"

We arranged that I would go to her house for eleven, had another coffee then left to get our respective buses home. My ankle was beginning to hurt so I wasn't too bothered about going back home so early and Katy said she wanted to make sure she had everything she needed for the meal.

"I'll ring you later," I shouted as her bus pulled away.

"Ok…see you tomorrow," she replied blowing a kiss.

I was thrilled to bits at the prospect of our meal together the following day – especially so as we had the house to ourselves.

Once back home I ran a deep bath and had a long soak. Just as I entered my room, with my thoughts very much on what had happened back in the barn, he spoke.

"God that was fantastic. I don't know how I stopped myself from yelling out loud when it happened. I hope you're appreciative, Gordon, of the fact that I controlled myself and behaved like a proper gentleman."

I was stunned into silence as it dawned on me what he was talking about. 'Oh no…he was there all the time…he'd seen it all…no, no, he'd experienced it all. Oh God, Oh my God.' An overwhelming feeling of disgust welled up inside me. I lowered myself onto the bed and held my head in my hands. 'He was there…Simon felt everything that I felt.' I shuddered once again. It was just too much to take in.

"Oh come on Gordon…what did you expect? I'm part of you. It's a bit like the old song, 'Me and my shadow.' You remember it don't you? Only better."

I didn't speak a word but my mind was going like crazy. But then after five, maybe ten minutes I calmed down and reasserted the solution that I had come to previously, that there was no point in engaging him in any conversation and that the best thing to do would be to behave as though he didn't exist. I was going to blank him completely. So I stood up went to my desk took out my physics text book and began to read the section on thermodynamics. I was aware all the time that he was there prattling on, cajoling me, goading me but I resisted the temptation to engage with him. To my great joy and amazement, by the time that I'd read the first chapter he had gone silent. 'There we are.' I said to myself. 'Just ignore him for long enough and he'll give in…after all what can he possibly do?'

I felt great. I now had a weapon with which to fight him and with that realisation I relaxed – so much so that I closed my book, undressed, got into bed and went straight to sleep.

Chapter 6

I woke the next morning at eight fifteen. 'Plenty of time.' I thought and lay back thinking about yesterday. I felt elated, not just because of the forthcoming date with Katy but because of the victory, as I saw it, over Simon. And the more I went over it the more convinced I was that I had genuinely gained the upper hand. He didn't have the power after all that he had boasted about, and although my foot was still quite painful, it was with a light heart that I eventually got up.

"Good grief," exclaimed my mother. "It's still morning Gordon and its Sunday…where are you off to so early?"

I didn't want to tell her exactly what I was doing so I said that Katy and I were going out with some friends from school.

"Well take a key because your dad and I are going out later. We'll be back by tea time…will you be wanting some?"

"No thanks mum. It'll probably be nine-ish when I'm back. But I'll take a key anyway…just in case."

"Breakfast?" she asked opening the bread bin.

"What time is…ah only half nine. Sure, thanks mum…just some toast. I'll make it if you're busy."

"No, no…you sit down. I'll have some with you and no doubt your dad'll smell it and want some too."

We sat at the kitchen table for a while eating toast and jam, drinking tea and chatting.

"D'you know you've looked at that clock every few minutes Gordon. There must be something special going on," she said with a mischievous sideways glance.

"Just a day out with my friends, Mum," I said nonchalantly, but I guess my reddening neck gave me away somewhat.

"Mmm I believe you…thousands wouldn't"

At ten fifteen I left the table, collected my jacket and left the house.

It was a dull but warm day and I had plenty of time to walk the three miles to Katy's house. When she told me where she lived I knew it straight away. It was a longish two bus journey but through the side roads and across the park it would be quicker to walk, especially so as it was a Sunday. The roads were almost deserted and I saw only three other people, two of whom were walking their dog and the third meandering rather unsteadily from lamp post to lamp post. The next right turn would bring me into Katy's street. It wasn't a long street but it was wide and lined with large trees, beech or maybe lime; I wasn't sufficiently knowledgeable to distinguish. The houses were semi-detached, large and set

well back from the road each with a short drive-
way which divided at the top, one branch leading
round to the side of the house and the other leading up to the front door. When first built they
would have been for the new upper middle
classes of the late Victorian era, but latterly the
area had become fairly run down with many of
the them having been split into flats.

I found the house easily and ran up the flight
of stone steps to the front door. It was the original
four panelled solid wooden one, and it even had
the tiny ornate letter slot and knocker set into the
frame. I knocked, rather too vigorously I thought,
judging by the great hollow boom that resounded
inside and down the hall. The old wobbly brass
door knob turned and the door swung slowly
open. Katy, dressed in an enormous deep blue
jumper and jeans, greeted me with a warm smile.

"Hi, come on in," she said softly as she stepped
back.

"Hi," I replied, suddenly unsure how to react
towards her on her own territory so to speak.

"Come on…its fine honestly," she assured me,
extending her hand to lead me in.

I stepped into the large vestibule and followed
her through the beautiful stained glass doorway,
down to the end of the long dark hall and right
into the lounge – or back parlour as it once would
have been called. It was so big that it would have

accommodated virtually the whole of the down-stairs part of our house.

"Wow!" I exclaimed as I gazed round open-mouthed.

The room was gigantic and full of original plasterwork - cornices and mouldings, many of which unfortunately were in need of repair.

"Mmm, I know what you're thinking…it's a mess. Dad's not hot on DIY."

"Yeah…I mean no, but it's fantastic…absolutely fantastic."

"Get away," she said incredulously.

"No honestly, I love this kind of thing," I replied, still trying to take it all in.

"Oh this place is just full of it. Anyway, d'you fancy a drink… coffee?" she asked leading me through another door into the kitchen.

I sat down at the massive table in the centre of the equally impressive kitchen. The place had been virtually untouched since it was built save for the odd lick of paint now and then.

"This house has been in my dad's family since nineteen nought plonk and nobody's had the interest, skill or money to do anything other than the essentials."

"Cor I wish I had a place like this," I said mesmerized.

"Oi, yoo-hoo, it's me you've come to see," said Katy waving the tea towel in front of me,

"Oh I know that but this place is something else. Anyway what've you made for our meal chef?"

"Just you wait and see. How's your foot by the way? It doesn't seem to be bothering you much."

To be honest I'd been so excited about getting there that I'd hardly given it a thought, but now that I was relaxing I became aware of the ache.

"Oh its fine thanks…just a twinge now and then."

As I was lifting the cup to my lips I looked up just as she was looking over the rim of her cup. Our eyes met. In the electric silence of the seconds that followed, my stomach flipped and my head began to swim. Then as though on cue we put our cups down on the table and stood up. My arms moved as if by themselves as I reached out for Katy's hands. Holding them tight I drew her to the side, away from the table and towards me. She withdrew her hands from mine and placed her arms around my neck. I encircled her waist with mine as she looked up into my eyes. Our lips met, at first gently but then more and more hungrily. I was crushing her to me eager to experience more and more of her – her warmth, her taste, the perfume of her hair, I was intoxicated. But then she pulled away and, holding me at arm's length, said with a teasing smile

"Well there's someone else who's pleased to see me," referring to that part of me that was pushing hard into her thigh.

"Oh Katy, you're driving me mad… ever since I first saw you I…I."

We kissed again softly, passionately and in one of the few times that we broke apart she told me that she had had her eye on me for some time.

"God I must have been blind," I growled.

With a thudding heart that felt fit to burst at any minute I found the bottom of her jumper and, holding my breath, ran my hands up the inside of it. Her skin was so soft and warm. Katy let out a squeal of delight as I, with a deftness that surprised me, unfastened her bra. But then she stopped me.

'Oh hell,' I thought, 'I've gone too far.'

I was mortified. What should I do? But then she smiled - a breathless nervous kind of smile

"No… not here… upstairs," she whispered.

All interest in the architectural delights of the place dissolved as we rushed headlong up the stairs and along the landing towards her bedroom. Closing the door behind me she began quickly to undo my trousers as I tugged with fumbling fingers at her jumper. We staggered across the room and fell onto the bed in total disarray rolling over and back, locked in a fierce and finally naked embrace.

Then it happened. My mouth opened and words came out but it was not my voice and the words did not originate from my consciousness. It was a bestial noise that I was powerless to stop.

'No Gordon, go down...go down. Kiss her there...oh yes, oh my God yes...down there...down...aaaaggghhh.'

The cry of ecstasy as I climaxed reverberated round the room. Katy froze, her eyes bulging from their sockets as a look of utter disgust rampaged across her face. I almost choked as I tried in vain to prevent the outburst. Then it went quiet and for a split second I thought it was over. I remained half kneeling between Katy's legs not daring to look at her or even move. But then I felt it again. It was as though something was inside me, some terrible force that I was totally powerless to control.

'Gordon go on...go on again...again. Oh Gordon just look at her oohhh aaaaggghhh.'

I tried to scream, to stifle my cry of ecstasy, to counter the vile noises that were coming from my throat. As the whole grotesque scene was unfolding Katy seemed frozen, just watching, stricken with horror. But then seconds later she opened her mouth screaming and yelling, lashing out with her fists and feet until I was on the floor.

"What...what did you say? Get off me. Get off me you bloody fucking creep. Get off...get out. Get out. Get...out."

When her voice gave out and she could scream no more she threw herself back onto the bed, pulled the cover over herself and sobbed bitterly.

I was stunned. My mind was numb. As I staggered and hopped around, trying to get dressed whilst at the same time trying to speak, all I could hear was Katy sobbing and every so often a voice, distraught and weak saying over and over, "Go...just get out."

Once dressed I stood for a second in the doorway, desperately wanting to go back but knowing full well that it would be useless to try to say anything. So I turned and left. I staggered downstairs and out onto the street in a complete daze. Once outside, as if the pain and despair over what had just taken place were not enough, I felt that the sky itself, dark and menacing now, was about to fall upon me and smother the last spark of life from my pulverised mind. I meandered through streets and back streets with no thought as to where I was going; my mind still numb, yet racing round and round in a vortex of blind panic. I may well have been a candidate for committal to a mental institution for that first half hour after leaving the house, but gradually the sense of utter chaos began to subside. In its place an overwhelming and blazing anger welled up and when it dawned upon me as to who was the target of that anger it grew into a rage of such magnitude that I felt I would literally be crushed by it.

At that very instant of revelation - when it became crystal clear as to what, or rather who was responsible, the voice, Simon, spoke. It was loud and triumphant, and it cut me to the very heart.

"You see…you see…I told you I'd do it. I knew that I'd win in the end…ha ha ha ha…"

The laughter went on and on growing louder and louder.

I shuddered to a halt and slumped against a garden fence as though pole-axed. Passers-by were commenting and giving me a wide berth as they went.

"Just look at him…drunk at this time of day…should be ashamed of himself."

After a couple of minutes or so I felt the strength begin to return to my limbs. I braced myself against the fence and stood up straight. I looked down at my hands and flexed my fingers and then gripped one hand with the other. Then throwing my head back I took great lungfuls of the cool refreshing air; one, two, three – deep, deep draughts. Slowly, very slowly I began to gather my thoughts and a glimmer of clarity was beginning to steal its way through the boiling, murky waters of my mind. Simon had to go, that much was obvious, but how? The thought grew and grew until it was all that I could think of, and I knew somehow that the first step was to get back home. Once there I believed that the next step would be made plain. Though still very disorientated I made my way slowly and painfully back.

The house was empty; it was after all still only early afternoon and my folks would not be back until much later. I walked steadily up to my room and went straight to the mirror at the side of my desk. I began to shake as I looked into it, sensing, but without knowing the reason, that it was a very significant thing to do. Struggling desperately to control myself I opened my mouth to speak. But before I could utter a syllable the voice of Simon got there first – loud and insolent.

"What are you looking at?"

After a brief silence which saw me reeling once again, he spoke for a second time now with even more confidence – goading me.

"Well? What about it…now who's in charge…not so bloody sure of yourself any more, are you Gordon?"

This last remark caused something to snap inside. Opening my eyes wide I peered even more intently into the mirror, as if to study the reflection in minute detail. Was I kidding myself or were there more than two eyes looking back at me? I don't know. I could have imagined almost anything at that point.

"What the…what are you looking at?" exclaimed Simon now not quite so assured.

I detected this slight change in his voice.

"I don't...I think...I...." I said hesitantly, thoughtfully as I looked closer and closer, scrutinising the reflection. "I'm looking for clues," I added finally. I was almost talking to myself by this time.

"What d'you mean... clues...clues for what?" he said defiantly.

I stayed quiet for a minute. And I don't know how or why but during that minute, it was as though a million synapses in my brain began firing, linking cell to cell – and the very first inkling of what was going on began to dawn.

"Clues as to what sort of... thing you are so that I can find out how to get rid of you once and for all," I said.

I now felt icy cold and my mind was clearer than I have ever known it to be.

"Humph...you can't do that. You don't know where I am...you hardly know anything about me."

These were bold words I thought, but from a now tangibly nervous Simon.

'Ping,' that's just what it felt like, as though the last crucial synapse connected.

"I'm getting rid of you Simon. I'm...getting ...rid...of...you... now, once and for all."

Now it was as though I was in a dream, but a dream over which I had full control. I was still icy cold, and totally calm. I knew what I must do and somehow Simon too must have realised that something drastic and final was about to happen. The voice in my head began to scream and plead.

"Gordon stop. You can't. Please don't…please I beg you Gordon… PLEASE… PLEASE… PLEEEAAASSE."

The infernal cries went on and on but I could shut them out. Don't get me wrong I was terrified but it was as though I was now on automatic and nothing could have prevented me from doing what I had to do.

Slowly I turned from the mirror, left my room and made my way along the landing to the stairs. The oddest thing about it was that as I made my way downstairs I began to hum 'Onward Christian Soldiers,' of all things. I found myself having to hum louder and louder as I approached the kitchen in order to drown out the cries and screams of terror within my head. But once there they stopped and were replaced with the most piteous pleading.

"Gordon…please. I'm sorry…please don't. pleeeaaasse. GORDON!"

I stood stock still. I'd decided that I would not engage in any conversation whatsoever with Simon and I was utterly inured to his pleas. I walked across to the oven housing and slid the four inch paring knife from the block on the worktop next to the hob. I sat on the floor in the far corner by the back door, lifted my shirt which still carried Katy's fragrance, and placed the point of the blade against my skin just enough to indent it slightly.

"Goodbye Simon, Goodbye Katy...my love," was all I said.

Tears filled my eyes as I took a deep breath and plunged the blade deep. I don't remember any pain; I don't remember anything else.

Chapter 7

So there I was in a hospital bed, linked to an array of instruments knowing that, for some reason which was unclear to me then, I had stuck a knife into myself while I sat on the kitchen floor. I looked at the clock on the wall – six fifteen.

I heard a clattering noise outside my room and a nurse came in. She checked the instruments and looked at me. She was young and pretty, and from her features I'd say from a far eastern country – Malaysia or Indonesia perhaps. But when she spoke her accent was decidedly western, quite cultured in fact.

"Good morning Gordon. How are you feeling?"

I found it difficult to speak at first and it was quite a shock to hear an actual voice for some reason. I just looked at her.

"That's OK…don't try to speak if it's difficult. You've been through the mill a bit haven't you?"

My lips were dry and my mouth felt like the bottom of a parrot's cage. She must have seen the expression on my face because she reached over for the plastic water bottle placed the spout into my mouth and squeezed. It tasted like nectar.

"Thanks," I said much relieved.

"Your parents are here; they've been here all night…came in to see you a few times. I'll tell them that you're awake. The doctor will be round to see you a little later."

She turned to leave after again checking the bag that was feeding a drip into my arm.

"Wait," I called. "Please…what's happened to me?"

"I don't know the details…I've just come on duty but, as I say, you'll have all your questions answered as soon as the doctor arrives. Now just you settle down again and rest."

As she opened the door to leave I noticed that there were two or three people outside in the corridor. I'm convinced they were looking in at me and one of them was pointing. The nurse seemed to shoo them away as she left and as the door closed I could hear whispered questions with lots of 'oohs' and 'aahs.' I felt a bit like a specimen – something of an oddity. I must have dozed off again because when I next opened my eyes two hours had passed and to my great surprise my mum and dad were there. They both looked tired out and it was obvious that they had been crying. My mum burst into tears afresh and knelt at the side of my bed holding my hand.

"Oh Gordon…Gordon," she wept.

My dad took her by the shoulders and gently drew her back to the seat.

He smiled a gentle smile.

"You gave us quite a fright there, Gordy," he said, his voice uncharacteristically soft and decidedly shaky.

I smiled back and urged them not to worry – I'd be fine. What struck me was the fact that as we spoke for the next ten minutes or so neither of them asked me why I had done it. It was as if they knew something that I didn't. Just then a tall slim man, I would guess in his late forties, entered the room. He acknowledged my mum and dad and then came to the other side of my bed.

"Right, Gordon. How are you this morning?" he asked in a strong Scottish accent.

The name on his badge read, 'Mr Andrew Macallister.' I gathered from this that he was some sort of surgeon.

"I'm pretty well… OK thanks," I replied. I looked from him to my parents then back to him, waiting for someone to tell me what had gone on.

"OK," he said drawing up another chair and sitting alongside the bed. "Your mum and dad know something of what it's all about but not everything. I was waiting till you were ready before telling you. Are you sure you're feeling up to this."

I was beginning to get exasperated with all the secrecy and mystery that I seemed to have attracted.

"Honestly…please go on," I urged.

"Well," he began. "When you came in yesterday afternoon it wasn't at all clear just what you'd done other than the obvious. It was quite apparent that it was an emergency and you were taken straight to theatre. When we managed to take a look inside we realised that there was more to it than anyone could have imagined and we had to call in quite a team…including a neurosurgeon and myself a vascular surgeon. You were in theatre for almost six hours."

I looked across to mum and dad who were goggle eyed at what they were hearing.

"I'm not exaggerating when I tell you that no one in that theatre had ever seen anything like it. What we found, and it was deep inside your abdomen virtually sitting on your main artery – the aorta, was a fully developed brain."

My stomach lurched at this revelation and my mother looked as though she was about to pass out. My dad just mouthed, "My God."

Mr Macallister continued.

"There were a number of other bits and pieces of tissue in the vicinity – which I won't go into detail about - but after much deliberation and discussion we concluded that what we had was the most unusual case of a rare condition known as Foetus in foetu."

He broke off and asked my mother if she wanted to break for a while as she was looking none too good.

"No...no. please go on. Could I just have a drink of water?"

She took the drink and Mr Macallister continued.

"It is the case that sometimes, in fact very rarely, during pregnancy where there are twins; one of them becomes absorbed into the body of the other. Usually there is no evidence of the absorbed one other than a few remnants and these would never come to light unless the surviving twin had surgery. But in this case...well there it was...the perfectly formed brain of a young adult."

I shuddered involuntarily as revulsion welled up within me. But this initial reaction soon abated as revelation dawned and things began to fall into place regarding Simon.

At that precise moment my attention was drawn to my mother. Her face was white and her expression, at first one of incredulity, slowly changed as if a distant glimmer of something once hinted at was just beginning to make sense. She turned to dad and said just one word.

"Simon?"

"Sorry... who's Simon?" said Mr Macallister turning to face mum who was by this time watching dad's mouth as he too whispered the name.

Mum took a deep breath and began to tell Mr Macallister the story of Simon as she knew it.

"Hang on mum," I broke in after a minute or so. "I think I need to do this."

And haltingly, over the next half hour I told them everything – well almost everything.

"My goodness gracious…oh my goodness… what an amazing story. So you came to the conclusion that Simon… was actually…inside you and that's why you…did what you did. My God, my God," he said over and over shaking his head in disbelief. "This must not go unreported. If it's alright with you I'd like to document everything you've told me…get everything down when you're up to it of course. Would that be OK?"

"Sure…why not?" I said, looking from mum to dad and back, not so much for their assent, more to reassure them that I was fine about it.

"Right then I'll leave you together…I'm sure you've a lot to talk about. Don't tire him out though eh?"

Mr Macallister shook dad's hand and squeezed mums arm reassuringly before leaving.

Over the next few days my recovery went well. I spent a long time piecing together and relating the whole story to the medical team that had been involved. It would be true to say that not one of them would have believed it if they had not seen it for themselves. The brain that was removed had been sent to pathology for study and found to be perfectly formed with the fully developed cortex of a young adult.

I must admit to feeling sorry for Simon and for the rest of my life I would refer to him as Simon, never just 'it' or 'the brain', after all we had shared so much.

Most of all I longed to see Katy and explain everything; perhaps in a little while I would write to her.

On the afternoon of the fifth day after the operation I was asleep in the dayroom. I had been up and about walking and it had exhausted me. I became aware that there was someone nearby and then felt warm breath followed by a soft kiss on my cheek. Opening my eyes I saw a silhouetted figure standing in front of me. I tried to speak but felt a cool finger tip on my lips and heard a beautiful and familiar voice.

"Sshh, don't say anything. I know all about it. Your mum found my number and called me…she told me everything."

I could not hold back the tears.

"I'm so sorry Gordon," she struggled to say through her own tears.

"Oh Katy, Katy no… no, there's nothing to be sorry about. You're here now and that's all that matters."

She sat on my lap and we stayed curled up together on the chair until the staff nurse came by and suggested that my stitches would heal a lot quicker without Katy sitting on them.

A week later I was discharged. Katy came along with my mum and dad to collect me.

It was a wonderful feeling as I waved goodbye to the place in which I had been reborn. There was just the tiniest niggling doubt in my mind though. It was something that Mr Macallister had said about the body possessing a remarkable, and little understood ability to disseminate memory throughout itself.

But I was not going to worry about that; for now I was going to enjoy my new found freedom, freedom to be myself alone.